Ghost Stories of Venice

From Historic Spanish Point to Englewood

By Kim Cool

HISTORIC VENICE PRESS

Ghost Stories of Venice

© 2002 Kim Cool

Historic Venice Press, P. O. Box 800, Venice, FL 34284

First Edition 2002
Printed in the United States of America
ISBN   0-9721655-0-9

Dedication

$\mathcal{A}$s one meanders along the twist-ed roads of life, and death, things happen, sometimes on schedule and sometimes when we least expect.

But everything that happens and everyone we meet, has some influence on the being that we become and the roads we choose to wander.

My road has been picturesque from beginning to end, though not entirely without a few bumps to punctuate the good times.

Now, as I embark on yet another venture, as a fledgling story teller, I must thank those who guided me in this

direction, beginning with my late father, Herman Patmore, who made up wonderful new stories every evening at bedtime for his favorite child - me; my late husband, Kenneth Adams Cool Jr., who always encouraged my creative efforts, my daughter Heidi who patiently listened to fake English accents and other nonsense night after night as I made up stories for her when she was little. And then there have been special friends like the late Mary Abbott who came into my life on three different occasions when I needed a nudge in a new direction, my adopted family and close friends Chip and Carole Ludlow, Marianna Csizmadia who read all these stories and most of all, my newest friend, the one who suggested I write "The Ghost Stories of Venice," read my first attempts and the final copy, the world's most prolific writer of ghost stories, Charles J. Adams III.

Contents

Introduction.....................7
Indian spirits inhabit area..................15
Bone chilling screams from the graveyard...21
Historic Spanish Point...............25
Hermitage haunter......................29
Are ghosts deterred by progress?............37
Golden Beach haunting...................44
Hog haunter................................54
Ghost riders in the sky...................58
Haunted by the circus...................61
San Marco Hotel gains new guests........67
Lookout at the Outlook...................71
Hungry haunters...........................75
Closure....................................81
Back to school............................87
Red marks the spot.......................90
Not with my car you won't.................93
Ghost cowhand.............................96
Geronimo was a snowbird...................99
The snowbird returned....................101
Is it or is it not?.........................104
Is that all?.............................107
About the author.........................109
Acknowledgements.........................110
Bibliography.............................111

Decorative
panel repre-
senting the burial
of the dead, the passage of
the river Lethe after death and the ascension into heaven.

Introduction

Like those special friends mentioned in the dedication of this book, ghosts have made their presence known to me in mysterious ways since I was a little munchkin.

The first ghosts I remember were those in stories told to me by my father. I was probably 5 or 6 at the time. Night after night he would spin his mysterious yarns just for me. Some tales were recounted from his own youth and others were wonderful stories created on the spot, with twists and turns probably dictated by my childish reactions and

questions.

Then there were those other ghosts that children with too vivid imaginations can conjure up from a bathrobe hanging on a closet door or a bedspread fallen from the bed in an odd shape that resembles something — or someone.

In school and at the movies I met ghosts created by Edgar Allan Poe and others portrayed by Vincent Price. His rendition of Poe's "The Pit and the Pendulum" will never be bested. Sunday afternoons, my father and I listened to "The Shadow" on the radio. Radio is the perfect medium for ghost stories because even the best story can be enhanced with a little help from one's imagination.

When I made my first trip to Disneyland I met up with the famed inhabitants of the Haunted Mansion, saw the holographically generated images that danced around the banquet table in the mansion's great hall and marveled at the Yettis on the Matterhorn ride.

Diehard investigators of the paranormal — those so-called ghost buster types — would scoff at these man-made images, discounting them as so many manufactured figments of some designer's imagination.

Or, were they?

Consider a world without mystery, a campfire without scary stories and

8

marshmallows, theater without Dickens' "A Christmas Carol" and other mysteries, or a library without the works of Poe.

Most stories, even the wildest works of fiction, derive from some grain of truth or experience. There have been ghost stories and other legends as long as there have been people to tell them, hear them, fear them and even to discount them.

Ghosts even haunt the hallowed halls of academia.

Sweet Briar College, my alma mater, has several. Most often seen or sensed have been the ghosts of Daisy Williams who was 16 when she passed on in 1884 and her mother Indiana Fletcher Williams who died in 1900. Sweet Briar was founded in Daisy's memory in 1901. Daisy's ghost seems more mischievous than that of her mother who seems to have continued to maintain a vital interest in her college.

No wonder the fascination with the supernatural endures. There have been enough confirmed sightings of "something" or "someone" and enough mysterious sounds that are more than just creaky steps, that even the most diehard skeptic would be hard-pressed to deny that, on occasion, things occur for which there seems to be no logical explanation.

Despite my own fascination with things that go bump in the night, my first message from "the other side" did not arrive until just after the death of my husband. After 14 years of enduring too many medical problems for any one person, Ken died, at the age of 51.

The message came to me shortly after the funeral, delivered by my cousin's husband Crayton, with a noticeable hesitation in his voice. We had returned to my house following the funeral service.

"There is something I must share with you," Crayton said. "While the minister was speaking, I was very aware of something — I don't know how to describe it — but something in the corner of the room. It appeared to rise and fall in rhythm with the minister's words. I don't know what it was but I sensed Ken's presence somehow. When the minister stopped speaking, whatever it was vanished."

Ken's body had been cremated. The remains were in a walnut urn, in the corner of the room described by Crayton.

My friend, Iona, had overheard the conversation.

"It was Ken," she said, matter-of-factly. "You always go to your own funeral."

She is a believer in ghosts and the supernatural and not afraid to admit it.

Crayton, on the other hand, is an engineer by training, a person who looks at things from the viewpoint of a scientist or mathematician, or, at least he did, until that day.

If Ken did appear at his funeral as Iona believed, and he wanted me to know that he was there, he chose well in appearing to Crayton.

One week later, on our daughter's birthday, Ken may have made one additional appearance. I had given his watch to Heidi. She took it off only to shower.

On her birthday, and at precisely the hour of his death, the alarm on his watch sounded. Was that a final birthday gift from her father? We like to think so.

Whether that was a message from the beyond or not, there is plenty of mystery in life, as well as in death.

Consider for a moment the people who have come into your life at one time or another, and then may have moved on but not passed on. Very much alive, these people may have gone elsewhere to impact other lives as they may once have impacted yours or mine.

Such encounters have led me into the needlework

business, the judging of figure skating, competitive curling, travel writing and, most recently, to hunt for ghosts and legends in my adopted community of Venice, Florida.

That Venice is not rife with famous haunted houses and other mysteries has made my hunt all the more interesting.

In the process I have learned that Venice is far more than just the Shark Tooth Capital of the World.

Although the prehistoric fossilized sharks teeth are not without mystery, there is far more to the history of this charming little beach town and its citizens who have come here from so many other places and times.

It was a chance meeting with another writer from another place that spawned my fascination with the other history of Venice, the other worldly history.

This first book of ghost stories and legends of Venice is a result of that encounter.

Was it only a chance meeting? I no longer think so.

As you meet some of the kindred spirits of Venice and its neighboring communities within these pages, you may agree.

To the best of my ability, I have related only true and verifiable tales. Some were told to me in the first person and some of the mysteries were report-

ed in the press at the time they occurred. Second hand tales sent me scurrying to my history books and to the city archives in an attempt to find a relationship between the story and some possibly related incident in the history of Venice. Given the preponderance of naysayers in these parts, most of these tales would never have found their way into this book except for the generosity of the story-tellers who were willing to share their tales.

That too is a common thread experienced by those of us who would pass on tales of the other side. Some people are truly afraid to even contemplate the reality of ghosts and want no part of such stories. Others think it is all make believe. Perhaps reality is somewhere in between.

So, fix a pot of tea, curl up in a favorite chair and take a different look at the Shark Tooth Capital of the World, one of the finest planned communities in America, a city that might have become a ghost town more than once except for its spirit — or spirits.

Photo by Kim Cool

The graves of Jesse Knight (1817-1911), at left, and Rebecca Knight (1825-1901) are located along Pioneer Lane in the Knight Memorial Cemetery, the oldest burial ground in Venice. It dates to the 1880s. Currys, Higels, Lowes and other pioneer families also are buried in this cemetery.

Photo by Kim Cool

The Triangle Inn, home of the Venice Archives and Area Historical Collection, was listed on the National Trust for Historic Places Feb. 23, 1996. Built in 1927, it operated as a guest house or bed and breakfast in its early years and was moved to its present location in 1991.

Indian spirits

*T*he first spirits to inhabit what has become Venice were probably the spirits of the Calusa Indians who inhabited this coastal area of Florida long before the white man made his first appearance in a boat from Spain.

Just north of Venice, at Historic Spanish Point, and south of Venice, along Manasota Key, there are shell middens which hold the key to the life of the Calusas. In both places, present day residents have reported mysterious sounds and sights, most often at night.

In Venice, the ghost of an Apache was discovered by a woman who said she is a medium. She said she was in the house to deal with another entity and came upon "a little demon" that she said was an Apache warrior who was unhappy with the people dwelling on "his land." The medium said that the Indian did not realize that he was dead.

That Indian could well be one of the nearly 450 Apaches who were brought to Florida sometime after 1876 for confinement at Forts Marion and Pickens.

She added that there are several homes in Venice that change hands nearly every year, a fact she attributes to the houses being haunted, often unbeknownst to their owners who are simply uncomfortable in the houses for unrecognized reasons.

On Manasota Key, and in Englewood, south of Venice, two former residents of The Hermitage shared three haunting tales.

Artist Caroll Swayze and her mother Ruth are convinced that the main house at the Hermitage is home to a female ghost.

The main house and other buildings on the property, now owned by the county, are destined to become an artist retreat within the next few years.

The buildings are being totally renovated, stripped down to the wall studs, in some cases.

A second female ghost was seen by Caroll in what is thought to be the oldest house in Englewood, the Rinkard House.

A third spirit, also in the Englewood area, could be the oldest ghost of a white man in the area, possibly even the ghost of Juan Ponce de Leon, the famous Spanish seeker of the Fountain of Youth. Born in 1460, Ponce de Leon was given the right to find Bimini, supposed home of the Fountain of Youth, as a reward for service to Spain. Instead, he landed in North America on what he thought was an island.

He named the land Florida for all the flowers which he saw there and returned to Spain. Five years later, he returned with two ships and 200 men, landing on the west coast of Florida in the area of Charlotte Harbor. DeLeon and the men went ashore and were in the process of building a settlement not far from the present site of the Hermitage when Ponce de Leon was struck by the arrow of a Calusa warrior. He was taken back to the ship which sailed to Cuba. He died there in July of 1521. However, his search in the area was never completed. Perhaps he continues to seek the coveted fountain.

That could explain several unexplained occurrences in the area.

Less than 20 years later, another famous Spanish explorer, Hernando de Soto, arrived with an armada of 10 ships and some 600 men, including many adventuresome noblemen from Castille. They sailed in seven large Spanish galleons, one highly maneuverable caravel and two brigatines.

The brigatines could be either sailed or rowed and, drawing just three feet of water, were ideal for exploring the shallow waters along the coast. Sailing by way of Cuba, de Soto landed at Charlotte Harbor, very near to where Ponce de Leon had been attacked by the Calusas.

From there, he moved north, founding the area now called Sarasota, and discovering the mineral springs at Safety Harbor, site of the Safety Harbor Spa near Tampa. It is said there are several spirits who regularly cause mischief there. I was there on a weekend when the spa was beset by several disturbances late one night. De Soto continued north from Safety Harbor toward Louisiana. Reaching the Mississippi River in 1541, he fell ill with a fever and died there on May 21. His body was first buried there, but was then dug up, wrapped in blankets, and sunk in the Mississippi lest his corpse be stolen by the Indians.

De Soto's spirit also may have returned to this tropi-

Photo by Kim Cool
One ghostly track is all that remains alongside the old Venice Depot at 303 E. Venice Ave.. Built in1927 by the Brotherhood of Locomotive Engineers, at a cost of $47,500, the Mediterranean Revival-style building is being renovated, at an estimated cost of $3 million, for its incarnation as a bus transfer station for the county system.

cal area, possibly to Sarasota for both the city and the county honor his name.

The west coast of Florida would remain a wilderness for some 300 more years before homesteaders would finally arrive to settle the area that would become known as Venice. The home-steaders were drawn by promises of free land and newspaper accounts of the beauty and the climate.

By the 1880s there were Knights and Higels and Roberts in the area and in 1888 settler Frank Higel named the area Venice because the many waterways reminded him of Venice, Italy. It had first been called Horse and Chaise because, from the water, the tree forma-tion reminded one of a horse and chaise.

With the arrival of the wealthy Chicago widow, Bertha Honore Palmer, in the early 1900s, and her purchase of some 140,000 acres, the future of Venice was secure. Palmer owned the largest cattle ranch in the state and a palatial home where she entertained wealthy northern friends who came to visit. While she did not live to see the devel-opment of Venice by the Brotherhood of Locomotive Engineers (BLE), the city would be built on Palmer lands sold by her sons Honore and Potter Jr. to New York orthopedic surgeon Dr. Fred Albee, who hired city planner John Nolen to create the ultimate retirement communi-ty for the BLE. When Albee sensed a

softening of the real estate market and sold his land and the Nolen plan to the BLE, he pocketed about one million dollars for his six months' work.

Venice was chartered by the state legislature in 1925 and incorporated as a city in 1927, not too long before the bottom dropped out of the real estate market. The city was well on its way to becoming a ghost town long before any spooks, goblins or things that go bump in the night would be reported in the area.

The town's population plummeted from 4,000 to 400 within months.

Finally, in 1932, the Kentucky Military Institute, seeking new winter quarters in Florida, arrived to save the city.

A further boost came in 1941 when the U.S. Army established an air base in Venice. World War II was heating up and several towns in Florida were selected to become military training bases. Venice, with its own airport and additional land that could be used for the new air base, was a prime spot.

By the time the war was over, the population had doubled, reaching 863 in the 1950 census but it would reach nearly 10,000 by 1957.

Beautifully landscaped, artfully planned and located directly on the Gulf of Mexico, it was only a matter of time before Venice would become worthy of haunting.

Bone chilling screams from the graveyard

What better place to find a ghost than in the local graveyard?

For years, even that was no easy task in the Venice area because there was no graveyard. Those passing on to their reward had to be taken to Englewood or Nokomis for interment, unless they were sent north, still a common practice because of the great number of people who come to Venice from somewhere else, primarily the Midwest or New England.

The Nokomis Graveyard, now known as the Knight Memorial Cemetery for early pioneer Jesse Knight and his family, is the eternal resting place of many of the earliest families of Venice. It is located not too far from the tracks of the old Seaboard Airline Railway which brought winter visitors to the area from 1911 when the tracks were completed until the early 1970s when passenger service south of Tampa was ended.

Since then, there has been little to disturb the residents from their eternal slumber.

Photo by Kim Cool

More recently, an unusual gravestone has made an appearance at the Knight Memorial Cemetery. Not adorned with cut out letters like every other stone or monument in this older graveyard, one stone appears lovingly hand-made. Each letter in the name of the deceased, Owen Marshall Rhines, was created of tiny coquina shells, most likely found on one of the near-by beaches where they are as plentiful today as they probably were in the early days when the earliest Knights trod the land. Rhines was born on May 20. 1913 and died on May 16, 1970.

Such peace was not the case in mid-March 1949. As reported in the *Venice Gondolier Sun's* March 15 edition, blood-curdling screams were heard emanating from the graveyard late one night. It was reported that the screams were from a woman and the local police were sent to investigate.

When they arrived, they found car tracks going over an unmarked grave.

They arrested a man named Leonard Benson the following Monday and accused him of damaging the graves, but the source of the screams remains a mystery to this day.

Perhaps the inhabitant of one of those graves did not like being disturbed in the middle of the night or, in the middle of a haunting?

There was no woman's name in the police report so, while it is possible that a woman might have been with Benson that night, and that she might have been the source of the screams, there is no record of it all these years later.

If she was in the car with Benson, did she scream because of something that he did, or because of something that the two of them might have seen in the old graveyard?

Only Benson, the unknown lady, and the residents of the graveyard know for sure.

Later that year, there was another ghostly event in Venice. It too was

reported in the Venice Gondolier Sun. That was the year that the fledgling Art Guild had purchased the old Venice Golf and Country Club, renaming it the Art Guild Country Club. The members of the new club held a large party in August of that year — a spook party.

When the guests arrived they were surprised to see a girl hanging from the ceiling above the bar, reclining on an upside down cot. She was covered in a few discreet places with moss and little else.

As the evening wore on, patrons of the bar became more and more convinced that she was real although they had been told that she was really a maniquin, made of plaster and paint. Real or not, she was the first Venice ghost to be written about in the local paper.

Today the site is home to Country Club Estates Mobile Home Park and there is a newer Venice Golf and Country Club, much farther east of the city. No ghosts have been reported in either place — yet.

Historic Spanish Point

Dating to about the same period as the Knight Memorial Cemetery is a much smaller burial ground.

Located at Historic Spanish Point in Osprey, just north of Venice, the tiny resting place for early settlers, the Blackburns, Webbs, Roberts and Guptils, is located on a small rise next to Mary's Chapel and within sight of Little Sarasota Bay.

Mary's Chapel is named for Mary Sherrill, a young woman who died while staying at the resort run by Frank and Lizzie Webb in the 1890s, at Spanish Point.

Mary's spirit, a vision in white, is a frequent visitor to both the chapel and to the White Cottage, according to neighbors of Historic Spanish Point and to several of the docents who volunteer their time at the site. She has been seen both in daylight and in the early evening. In the daytime, docents have seen her as they have led tours through the 30-acre site, usually hovering off in a wooded area, but close enough that she can listen to the

Mary's Chapel at Historic Spanish Point sits on a slight rise within sight of the bay that surrounds the point. Many early pioneers are buried in the adjacent cemetery.

docent's spiel.

When she has been seen in the early evening hours, the appearance has most often been noted near the water's edge, about where the White Cottage is located. It was built in 1884 and called "The Dormitory" by the Webbs and their resort guests. She probably stayed in the dormitory while a guest and continues to bide her time in that area.

It also is the building with the most wide-sweeping view on the property.

Although the most visible spirit and the only one with a name, Mary is not the only nocturnal visitor to this hallowed ground.

Long before the arrival of the Webbs, Historic Spanish Point was home to early Floridians who hunted in the area, cooked their food and buried their dead on the site. The burial mound and two shell middens that contain the evidence of these early Native American people, have been preserved for the education of present-day visitors.

There are several homes along the northern property line of the site and it is along this line that many of the homes' residents have reported strange sights and sounds late at night.

The sightings have all been similar — reports of shadowy wispy things floating through the trees. The sounds have been more identifiable, something akin to footsteps but softer and often

with a discernable beat.

Perhaps the sightings and the sounds echo from the spirits of the pre-historic Indians returning to check on the graves of their ancestors and on the status of the ceremonial offerings they left in the burial mound more than 1,000 years ago.

And, according to Venice artisan Trevor Charnley, stomping sounds are occasionally heard. He attributes those to Bertha Palmer, the doyenne of Historic Spanish Point, the lady who built The Oaks there as her winter home.

The main house is gone, destroyed in a fire in the 1950s, but her sunken garden, pergola and other buildings remain, as does The Oaks' name which is used to identify one of the most upscale developments in the area, with homes selling for $1 million and up.

One other spirit has a tie to Historic Spanish Point.

"Captain Taylor used to pilot his fishing boat from Spanish Point to Venice before the waterway was dug," Charnley said. "He sometimes sailed as far south as Englewood."

Charnley describes Taylor as a mis-chievous spirit who often shows up for services at the Church of the Angels in Venice.

Hermitage haunter

One of the last remaining Florida homesteads along the Gulf of Mexico is the Hermitage, on Manasota Key, just south of Venice.

The original house was built circa 1903 by Carl Johanson, an Englewood sawmill owner. He rafted the lumber across the bay to the site which faces the Gulf of Mexico.

Badly decayed and neglected for many years, the property was purchased in 1986 by the county and is destined for a new life as an artists and writers refuge. To that end it is being restored with grant money obtained by a consortium that includes the Sarasota County Arts Council and several public and private foundations and arts organizations.

The drive to save the property from being turned into a parking lot was begun years ago by a lady named Ruth Swayze. The house had fallen into a serious state of disrepair and was not only an eyesore in the neighborhood but also the scene of drug deals and other undesirable happenings.

She said that she had complained to the owners and, by a "fluke," to use her word, was offered the opportunity to live there for low rent in exchange for becoming the property's watchdog.

Soon after taking up residency she learned that a county commissioner was pushing to have the site turned into a parking lot. Vowing to prevent such a trav-

Photo by Kim Cool

Destined to become an artists' retreat, the Hermitage, at 6600 Manasota Key Road, Englewood, dates to 1903. It is being restored by a combination of grants from private groups and foundations and funds from the Sarasota County Arts Council. Artists will be free to pursue their work in the hauntingly inspirational setting, in return for sharing their expertise with members of the surrounding communities.

esty, she began her campaign.

"I had open houses every Saturday," Swayze said. "Parks and Rec owned it by then. They made it look nice but they didn't fix the roof. It eventually fell in, ruining the pecky cypress and heart of pine floors."

She had moved out of the house before the roof caved in, but continued her vigil and maintained her faith that the house would be saved. Swayze, her husband and her daughter had lived there nearly 12 years.

"It was the most magical time of my life," she said. "People just dropped in and they would stay for two weeks. Once we had 20 staying in the house, mostly writers and artists.

"There was always someone to play the piano.

"You knew you were safe at all times."

The Swayzes lived in the main house on the property, a big old house that had been built on a bluff close to the beach in 1905. It is believed to be the second oldest house on Manasota Key. The property is the site of a prehistoric Indian midden, an archeological testament to the native Americans who once roamed the area. In the 1930s, at the height of the naturalist movement, the property was the site of a nudist colony.

"My husband was rarely home at night because of his job, but I always

felt safe in that house," she continued. "Even when one of the former druggies would show up, I always felt safe."

Swayze may have felt so safe because someone or something was protecting her even as she was protecting the house.

"One day, a friend came to visit from New York City," Swayze said. "She brought another friend with her, a lady who supposedly was a psychic.

"That night, the guests went upstairs to sleep.

"The next morning when I got up I found them in the living room, one on each sofa.

"They couldn't stay up there. The psychic wouldn't even go back upstairs to get her things. I decided that they must have met my lady, a woman who was supposed to have been a healer, a grandmother.

"She could cure anybody. She would use tree bark and other things and it always worked and she is said to have had a lead stone (a crystal)."

Swayze said the lady was the mother of Dr. Alfred R. Whitney, an architect who had built the second house on the property back in 1941, a house that, even today, surpasses current building standards and is considered to be virtually hurricane-proof.

He also built two cisterns, four water systems, a pump house and garage on the property.

The elder Mrs. Whitney had moved on to another realm before the Swayzes moved in to the Hermitage.

Mrs. Whitney had been buried on the mainland, but her stone, the one that was thought to have healing powers, was said to have been buried somewhere on the property.

"It is assumed that that is why she had to come back," Swayze said. "Even if you don't believe in ghosts, she left something in that house - that feeling of almost rapture - if you were in the house at that time you would understand."

Swayze said that every year in the house was better

Photo by Kim Cool

Living room of the Whitney House at the Hermitage which, when restored, will house independent artists for residencies of four-six weeks to nurture new artistic achievement and culturally enrich the greater Venice-Englewood area.

than the preceding year.

Only one person ever saw "the person swishing past wearing blue," but Swayze said she always considered her presence, even when she was painting the house.

"I painted all the rooms in the colors they had originally been," Swayze said. "But I only painted half the kitchen because it seemed like something bad might happen to that house if I ever finished painting the kitchen.

"I'm half Irish, you understand, I painted the kitchen yellow even though I don't like yellow. I knew I would be OK if I didn't use a different color."

After the Swayzes moved out, the house was moved farther back on the property to its present location, In the process, a giant live oak tree was removed, to Swayze's distress.

At its original location, there was only one window in the house that did not offer a view of the water, Swayze said.

At its new location, the water can be see most easily from the second floor because the slight hill where the house once was located blocks the view from most of the main floor rooms.

What is uncertain is whether the spirit of the kindly grandmother moved with the house. No one has occupied the house since its move and no one will occupy the house until the extensive restoration work has been completed and the house is readied for its next role as an artist's retreat.

As Ruth Swayze was a writer and her daughter is a painter, the grandmotherly ghost in blue may not find the atmosphere all that different in the restored home,

Swayze's daughter Caroll, a graduate of York University in Toronto, was married on the property.

The site held two 20- by 40-foot tents with ease, she

said.

Also on the site is a prehistoric Indian midden, undisturbed for centuries, a veritable fount of information on the early people of the area.

Long before the lady in the blue dress appeared there were likely to have been Indian spirits at the hermitage and possibly the ghost of a Spanish explorer or two.

Perhaps the ghost of Juan Ponce de Leon stops by on occasion in search of the Calusa Indian whose arrow felled the famed Spaniard in 1851.

Or, his spirit may be a few miles to the south, in Indian Mound Park, along the water in Englewood where there are several additional middens left by Calusas who lived in the area from 1000 BC to 1350 AD. The largest mound in the park is believed to be a refuse mound (also known as a trash dump) but there are other mounds in which skeletal remains have been found.

Such mounds were created in many areas along the Gulf coastline but few remain because most development began on the coast and then moved inland, destroying any middens that were in the way.

Those few that remain, like those at the Hermitage and in Indian Mound Park, are on protected sites, at least for the foreseeable future.

Englewood itself, was not devel-

oped in the 1920s as Venice had been because the Seaboard Air Line Railway had not extended its lines to the area when the real estate boom ended. The big plans for Englewood's future remained on the drawing board for several decades.

The oldest house in Englewood, at 2 Englewood Road, at the corner of Dearborn Street, was a boarding house run by a Mrs. Quimby from 1897 until about 1912 when it was turned into a private residence.

Among those who lived in the home during the next several decades was the family of Andrew Jergens, inventor of Jergens lotion.

In 1949, the house once again became a guest house and was known as Mrs. Donna Rinkard's Guest House.

This old house, as the crow flies, is quite close to the Hermitage, but on a bay instead of the Gulf of Mexico.

Its connection with the Hermitage is not one of location, so much as one of family.

Sometime after Caroll Swayze was married, she moved from one oldest house to another, the Rinkard house, where she had the first of two haunting experiences of her own.

Caroll lived and worked in the house, maintaining a gallery on the first floor.

"A friend said that a woman used

Photo by Kim Cool

The Englewood Mound in Indian Mound Park was made by Calusa Indians who occupied Florida's southern Gulf Coast from 1000 BC-1350 AD. Mounds, called middens by archeologists, provide clues to the people who used them whether as trash heaps or burial grounds. Indian Mound Park is on Winson Street along the shore of Lemon Bay in Englewood.

Photos by Kim Cool
Ruth Swayze said she felt protected and safe from the minute she moved into the main house at the Hermitage where she resided for more than 12 years.

When artist Caroll Swayze lived in the old Rinkard house in Englewood, she saw one apparition but when she had her own gallery at 30 N. Elm St., she had a totally different experience with a mysterious presence that visited regularly and bid her adieu in a most unusual manner. Swayze is shown here in front of the Whitney house that was built at the Hermitage in 1941 and will one day house visiting artists in a retreat program run by the Sarasota Arts Council.

to come regularly to the house," she said. "She was a lady who lived in a trailer park nearby. She would go upstairs and cry. She was just overwhelmed by it and she came at least once a week."

Caroll said that things would come off the walls at night. Other things would be moved around and there was never a reason for any of these strange happenings.

Then one night, she was upstairs in the south bedroom, fast asleep.

She awakened sometime in the middle of the night to see someone at the foot of the bed.

"There was a woman there at the end of the bed," she said. "She was wearing some sort of diaphanous gown. It was a light color and her hair was very light or white even.

"She had her arms outstretched toward the window and looked as though she wanted to go through it."

Seconds later, she was gone.

Whether she went through the window or the wall, Caroll could not say.

She did not see the ghostly female again. Nor did she ever learn who the lady might have been.

But, whoever she was, she or an associate continued to move things about during the night.

Caroll eventually moved to another house and acquired a gallery in retail

space nearby.

The Rinkard House was vacated in the 1980s and sold at auction in 1992. For several years it had an uncertain future but is once again occupied.

Or maybe, the house has always been occupied — by something.

Caroll's second haunting experience occurred in her gallery at 30 N. Dearborn St. also in Engelwood and just a few blocks east of the Rinkard House. It is a tiny little Florida Cracker-style building beneath the spreading boughs of an ancient Live Oak tree.

Today the pink and white, wood frame building is used as a combination tea room and internet cafe.

While Caroll ran the gallery, which had several rooms, she had a regular visitor, one she never saw.

"Daily, I would hear the front door open and someone would walk into the purple room," she said. "Then they would turn right and go into the red room.

"You could hear their foot steps.

"I'd say 'Hello' and then there would be silence.

"One day, I said nothing but ran into the room.

"There was no one there.

"It was the same pattern, day after day."

Caroll said the visitor never went beyond the red room and it seemed as though they were just looking around, perhaps checking on something.

Tiring of being a "shop girl", and wanting to concentrate on her painting, Caroll decided to leave the gallery.

On the last day, as she was patching walls and carrying the last things out to the car, the mystery visitor returned.

"I heard it again and went into the big room," she

Photo by Kim Cool

The bedroom where artist Caroll Swayze was visited by the ghost of the Rinkard House, 2 Old Englewood Road, Englewood, is in the upper left.

Photo by Kim Cool

When artist Caroll Swayze had an art gallery in this building at 30 Elm St. in Englewood, she had a daily visitor. Who or what was never determined but on her last day in the gallery, she was able to find closure even as the back door was blown open by an unseen force. Today the building houses a tea room and internet cafe.

said. "There was no one there.

"The front and back doors were closed and latched and the windows were closed so no breeze could come from outside.

"Yet I felt this cold air around me.

"It gives me goose bumps to talk about it.

"I sat down on the floor in the middle of the room and said, 'What do you want?' There was a breeze around my ears and then there was a big wind blowing all around me. My hair was blown on end.

"Nothing was open.

"I said, 'I gotta leave, it is gonna be OK.' unsure who I was speaking to.

"All of a sudden, the back door flew open and the wind blew outside. It was such a presence I think I stayed on the floor for five or 10 minutes.

"It was more like an energy than an actual person."

Caroll said there was no way the door could have been blown open by the wind that she had experienced inside the house.

Not only was the back door securely closed and latched but — the door opened in as the wind went out.

Are ghosts deterred by progress?

In the middle of the 20th century, Venice was being reborn yet again.

The 1920s had been the years of the city's creation by the BLE. The 1930s were the years of its first reincarnation, thanks to the arrival of the Kentucky MIlitary Institute (KMI) and the 1940s were the years of the second reincarnation, spurred by the U.S. Army when it established the Army Air Base to train World War II fighter pilots.

After the war ended, boom times were about to descend on Venice yet again.

Perhaps the townspeople were too busy to notice any ghost(s) in those days.

Although there was at least one at the train station.

The depot ghost is a lady, patiently waiting for her lover to return from the war. Another lady who wishes to remain nameless said she has seen her on several occasions, waiting on the platform Perhaps one day, the one she awaits will find his way back to the station.

Meanwhile, the infrastructure that remained from the town's earliest days finally came back to life.

The old Worrell Apartments became the first site of Venice Memorial Hospital which opened in 1951.

A new Venice Yacht Club was created that same year and drama buffs petitioned the city for permission to use an empty airport hangar as the first home of the Venice Little Theater.

Within just a few weeks, volunteers had built a stage and produced "The Torchbearers," the first of three plays presented that inaugural year. These early years also saw the birth of the first Venice Public Library in Venice and the Venice Art League.

Dr. Douglas Murphy had a hand in the hospital and yacht club foundings and also in the development of Guaranty Bank, a new community bank in the still tiny town. Charles Finley and Geri Becker were among the early actors at the Venice Little Theatre. They remain active in the group today.

No decent ghost would have considered haunting the VLT's sorry little building in those days. To make sure, the fledgling thespians, honoring an old theatrical superstition, made sure the ghost light was lit at center stage whenever the theater would otherwise be dark.

Becker said that when it rained, the audience members had to pick up their feet while the water whooshed by under their seats during thunderstorms.

Cast and crew all shared one toilet in a stall behind the building.

It would be at least 20 years before the VLT had a theater fit for haunting and even today, no one has admitted to seeing a ghost there although VLT's executive director Murray Chase does acknowledge hearing plenty of strange sounds late at night in the cavernous building that has become the present and much grander home for the local thespians.

The present building was created from the old Orange Blossom Garage which housed the KMI gymnasium and armory from 1932-1970.

And today's theater guild membership is nearly as large as Venice was when the theater was born in the early 1950s. But today's thespians seem much less superstitious than the VLT pioneer actors.

There is still a ghost light but it is not the bare bulb of yore, Chase said. Perhaps that is why he has heard the sounds of things that go bump in the night in the little theater. And perhaps that is why two of the newest theater students are convinced that the theater is indeed haunted despite any bone-chilling evidence.

Two earlier mysteries haunted Venice in an entirely different manner.

The Tamiami Trail (U.S. 41), connecting the cities of Tampa and Miami had been completed years before the VLT was born but remained just a two-lane road. If one driver dawdled, everyone dawdled, or, grew impatient, leading to several speeding arrests that were chronicled regularly in the local paper.

The KMI, the nearly ideal climate and the Gulf beaches remained the biggest draws to potential new residents. Hauntings went unreported in those days.

Perhaps they were hushed up lest they deter new residents.

Mysteries on the other hand, were not hushed up and included several strange automobile accidents and even one murder.

One of the strangest auto accidents involved five older ladies who drowned in a car that ran off the Tamiami Trail and into Shakett Creek in the middle of the afternoon on March 9, 1949.

The weather and roads were clear when the women were hit from behind by a truck whose driver should have seen the big four-door Oldsmobile sedan. Following the impact, the driver of the Olds lost control, sideswiped a Packard and plunged into the water.

Rescuers were on the scene immediately but everything that could go wrong went wrong. The doors on the Olds were jammed and no one could open them. When the rescuers managed to hoist the car to the surface on a winch, it fell back as soon as it broke the surface of the water. Finally, someone dove into the water, smashed the windshield and managed to pull two of the ladies out and bring them to shore. But it was too late. Attempts at artificial respiration failed. All the ladies but one were widows. Perhaps their company was sought elsewhere.

In the next issue of the paper there was an appeal to build better guard rails along that stretch of the Tamiami Trail. The rails were not built and two

years later a very similar accident happened but with a different ending for the car's three occupants who were neither widows nor widowers.

Ray Higel, a descendent of Frank Higel, the man credited with giving the name of Venice to the city, witnessed this second accident, dove into the water, smashed the car's windshield and managed to save all three victims.

The mysterious murder happened on March 28, 1959. Mrs. Hazel O. Woodard, 51, was lying on the couch in her living room, watching television when someone shot her through the screened door of her home.

She was married to a former commissioner, W. L. Woodard of Laurel.

In the weeks following the tragedy, the police questioned everyone, including the husband. Clues were few and far between. They found the spent shell outside and one large footprint, but nothing else. The husband offered a reward and the papers kept the story in the public eye until an arrest was finally made on April 23.

An itinerant man named Norman Smith was arrested that day, nearly a month after the killing. He was a diagnosed schizophrenic and was immediately sent to the asylum for the criminally insane.

Whether Hazel ever managed to haunt and torment her killer is unknown.

Location, location, location

Neither a home's age nor location seem to matter when it comes to ghostly goings on.

If they did, this writer's hunt for hauntings would have been even more of a challenge than it was in this rather young Florida town by the name of Venice.

One of the newest Venice ghosts has only recently made an appearance in his former house although he died in 1977, at the age of 81. His passing occurred in the home's family room on August 20 of that year.

In deference to the man's heirs who still reside in Venice, the present homeowners have asked for anonymity for themselves and for the man we have agreed to call "the captain."

On the day he passed on, the captain had some sort of attack, and his wife called the neighbors for help. Although they came immediately, by the time they arrived in the house, the captain had already moved on to a different realm.

The different realm was not so far away, according to the home's present occupants. They also reported that water seems important to this particular spectre.

Perhaps the man had a water fetish.

In any event, the captain seems more creative than the average poltergeist. Or perhaps it is that he was first simply being reclusive. For it seems there are far more reports of sensations, smells and sounds than of sightings in the literature of ghosts and goblins and things that go bump in the night.

In the case of the captain, water was the medium used to announce his first few visitations.

As they did every night, the present homeowners locked the house, turned out the lights and went to bed, often being lulled to sleep by the sound of waves from the nearby Gulf of Mexico.

Usually they were gently awakened by the rising sun.

Until that first fateful night when the sound of running water disturbed their slumber in the middle of the night.

Arising from their bed, they discovered that every faucet in the house had been turned on. But instead of hearing a steady *drip ... drip ... drip,* there was a torrent of water gushing out of each and every faucet.

This happened on more than one occasion but always at night.

Plumbers were called in but they could find no earthly reason for the strange happenings.

Neither the plumbers nor the homeowners considered any other explanation.

A few weeks later, things escalated. In addition to occasional nighttime disturbances, the outdoor sprinkler system began to turn itself on for no reason. Again, the water was turned on full force but during daylight hours.

Again the plumbers were called and again there seemed to be no earthly reason for the watery phenomenon.

Nor did anyone suggest that there might be some other reason.

Yet, despite stepping up their vigilance in checking every faucet and light switch each evening before retiring for the night, the strangehappenings continued to occur, with no warning and on no set schedule.

But, there is more.

And it would take much more before this tale would be shared with anyone and before anyone would consider an otherworldly reason.

Consider that these mysteries were taking place in Venice, Florida, a town that had never been known for being haunted.

The second mysterious occurrence followed some weeks later.

The husband's mother came to visit. One afternoon, ailing with a severe migraine headache, she was relaxing in the family room, very close to the spot where the captain had passed on.

Shades of Poe, there came a tapping

51

and a not so gentle rapping on that chamber's wall. For endless minutes, the tapping and rapping continued, disturbing the poor woman's rest and worse yet, her psyche.

Investigation proved fruitless. There was no visible person or thing on the other side of that wall, nothing that might explain the disturbance.

Although she did not visit again for some four years, not even rapping and tapping on top of dripping would lead either of the home's occupants to consider that their home might be haunted.

The captain, while continuing to make his spirit felt, simply had to take more drastic measures before anyone would consider that he was the cause of the disturbances.

He had to make an appearance.

And even that was not quite enough for these two reluctant hauntees.

The mistress of the manor may have been the first to see the captain's spectre but, until she discovered a sympathetic listener, even she continued to be reluctant to mention any of the mystical mayhem in her house.

"It was not a white shadow," she said one afternoon. "I saw him go by the window on more than one occasion."

And only after telling this writer about the backyard visitation, did she finally share the tale with her husband.

She had been afraid to tell him for fear he would think her crazy or, at the very least, too wrapped up in the home's mysterious mishaps.

"Well, after telling him, he told me that he had not wanted to say anything, but he too kept seeing someone (something) during the same time period in the same place! I told him I was going to be in contact with you (this writer) and he is OK with it."

These two were not alone in their reticence to speak about possible paranormal experiences.

But once they found a nonjudgmental ear, their tale spilled forth, as the water had gushed from their faucets, followed by e-mail and telephone calls offering up additional information about what may be the most active ghost in Venice.

For there is still more to this particular haunting.

Recently, there was a second death in exactly the same spot in the family room where the captain left this worldly life behind.

"Our dog, Ginger, died on the exact same spot," the lady of the house said. "She had been ill and my husband was holding her when she died."

And then there were two.

Beware of
hitch-hiking ghosts

Spook Hill is a good two hours away and reports of haunted houses remain a rare commodity in Venice, but many residents were quick to share the story of the phantom motorcyclist of Center Road.

The mysterious motorcyclist is especially well-known to residents of Venice Gardens, the development just south of Center Road where the shadowy rider has been seen regularly since the early 1960s.

"When you headed east on Center, he would be right behind you, with a red light on his cycle," Laura Young Thurman said. "It would scare the pee willies out of you and the big dare was to leave you out there all alone."

Thurman is a 1977 graduate of Venice High School and now works as a mounted patrolman for the Oakland Police Department outside of San Francisco.

Her sister, Lisa Young, a U.S. Army helicopter pilot stationed in Alaska, and Venice undertaker David Farley, also knew about the ghost rider.

"He was often seen in the 1960s when I first came to Venice," Farley said.

Although Venice was on the grow again, there was not much for teenagers to do in the decades of the 1960s and the 1970s.

Like their bored counterparts out in California who cruised the Sunset Strip each evening, Venice teens also went cruising — out on Center Road, a street that was referred to as the "road to nowhere."

Venice Gardens was still new, and most of its homes were closer to Shamrock Boulevard, Thurman said. Streetlights were virtually non-existent in that area back then.

"Center Road was hardly paved in the 1960s," she said. "It went all the way to River Road but there was nothing from the bypass (U.S. 41 - Tamiami Trail) to River Road.

In those days, about all that was on Center Road was the Venice Gardens Community Center with its pool and

tennis courts. The center was closed after dark.

"We did a lot of monotonous U-turns," she said about cruising Center Road with her friends. "That red light was always there, always behind you, no matter which direction you were going."

Despite the growth spurt that resulted from this new development, Venice remained a sleepy little beach community and had yet to become an island.

The town had two airports for awhile (Albee Field and the Venice Army Base which later became the Venice Municipal Airport) but the ghostly rider seemed to be its only ghost in those days.

Perhaps he had to keep riding back and forth because there still was no cemetery in the immediate Venice area until Farley opened Venice Memorial Gardens later in the 1960s.

In attempting to learn his identity, this writer uncovered news of several motorcycle accidents in the vicinity of Center Road and Tamiami Trail during the 1950s.

The mystery rider could have been any one of these unfortunate souls but there is one other possibility that seems much more likely.

In the mid 1950s a man moved to Venice after retiring from an illustrious career as a motorcycle race pace driver.

The pace driver's name was Frank Jehan and he is said to have been one of the greatest pace riders on the circuit.

Jehan rode in races all over the world and was the winner of the Babe Ruth Challenge Cup and the Providence Golden Wheel among dozens of others.

Given the penchant for the motorcycling ghost to stay close to the drivers he was following, it seems quite likely that Jehan may have come out of retirement once he got to the "other side.

Photo by Kim Cool

Several motorcycle riders will spend their eternity at Venice Memorial Gardens on Center Road, the road well traveled by the ghostly cyclist in the accompanying story.

Ghost riders in the sky

The year was 1967.

In April, two residents on Alhambra Road spotted mysterious round object in the sky above the Venice Beach. Alhambra runs primarily east and west, changing its name to the Esplanade when it turns to run along the beach.

The residents, Mrs. C. Lawrence Vickers and Mrs. Roy Priest, both lived in the 600 block of Alhambra. They reported the sighting to a reporter for the Venice Gondolier Sun and said they watched the object for some time as it hovered over the beach. Suddenly it veered off into the western sky out over the Gulf of Mexico.

Construction of the Intracoastal Waterway had been completed some months earlier, making an island of

Venice.

While some residents worried about being cut off from the fire department which was located on the mainland, the town was booming. Condos were being built along the beach, new homes were going up in record numbers every year and architect Edward Seibert of Sarasota was chosen to design a permanent home for the Venice Art League.

Perhaps, the passengers in the UFO were considering a move to Venice, despite the city's stop and start history.

Even Venice Gardens, now cut off from the beach by the Intracoastal, was nearing build out.

Three bridges provided access to the new island which also was home to the Greatest Show on Earth, the Ringling Bros. and Barnum and Bailey Circus. The circus had moved its winter headquarters to the Venice Arena, located on airport property, in 1960. Many of the circus stars made their homes in Venice. It was not unusual to see acrobats and aerialists practicing their tricks in their yards.

A man riding a bicycle along the road might turn out to be something entirely different when viewed in the rear view mirror by the driver of the car that passed him — a man with a pasty white face and grotesque lips and eyes — not a ghost, but a budding circus clown, studying his art at Clown

59

College in Venice.

The cemetery is on Center Road, the road frequented by the motorcycling ghost referred to in the previous chapter.

Oddly, references to that ghost seemed to dwindle about the time the cemetery began to be more populated.

Perhaps he finally had a place to park his cycle.

And, perhaps one of those creatures with a pasty white face and grotesque lips and eyes was not a clown after all.

Read on.

Venice remains
haunted by the circus

Like much of Florida during the frenzied Florida land boom of the 1920s, Venice was a circus.

Years later, a quieter and less populated Venice would become the winter quarters for several circuses, including the biggest one of all, The Ringling Bros. and Barnum & Bailey Circus. The Greatest Show on Earth wintered in Venice from 1961 until 1992.

And always, when a circus is in town, there is at least one ghost, one that, until now, only the performers knew about.

This ghost would make weekly appearances, dispensing $2 bills by the pound.

His welcome presence would be announced by the

words, "The ghost is riding."

"That's a circus term," a former performer told me at a gathering of Show Folk of America, in Sarasota. "It meant it was payday but no one else would know what it meant."

In Venice, the $2 bills were used by the circus pay-master at the suggestion of John Ringling, so that the city's business owners would realize the positive eco-

Once bedecked with huge signs proclaiming it to be the winter quarters of The Greatest Show on Earth, the Ringling Bros. and Barnum & Bailey, the Venice Arena lived a somewhat quieter life in its fifth decade. The building was custom-built for the most famous circus in the world when it moved to Venice in 1961. Since the circus left in 1992, the arena has been used for a variety of businesses and has hosted professional boxing matches within and skateboarding contests in its back lot where the menagerie tent was erected.

nomic impact of the circus.

The show maintained its winter quarters in Venice for 31 years until crumbling railroad tracks made it too dangerous to bring the huge circus train into town. When neither the city fathers not the Seaboard Air Line Railway was willing to spend the money to repair the tracks, the death knell was sounded and the aging circus arena was vacated.

But the spirit of the circus remains to this day, and so do a great many circus performers who continue to make their homes in Venice.

At least one spirit of another variety may also remain in Venice.

He first appeared late one evening according to a tale shared by Penny Wilson, who like her father, Dime Wilson, and other family members before and since, had an animal act. Members of the Wilson family have been in the circus business for 300 years she said. They have had bear acts, chimpanzee acts, horse acts, tiger acts and recently, a grandson started a mixed cat act.

The mysterious spirit experienced by Dime appeared in the menagerie tent at the Venice circus grounds in the early years of the Ringling show's stay in Venice.

It happened late at night, long after the day's rehearsals had ended.

"Something had spooked the ani-

mals," she said. "My father went into the tent to check on them. Though the night air was warm for that time of year, he felt a cool breeze on his neck."

The animals were restless but as he wandered through the tent, he saw nothing and no one.

Yet the chilling breeze followed him and then — someone, or something, slapped him.

"There was no one there but him and the animals," Penny repeated.

Not only did Dime feel the slap. He heard it, and so did the animals.

At the sound, the animals became so agitated that some of the horses actually broke loose and bolted from the tent, she said.

The next day, the animals were all back in the menagerie and in true show-must-go-on tradition, the show did go on.

The mysterious visitor never returned.

Perhaps he (or it) remains on the circus grounds, patiently waiting in the wings for the circus itself to return to Venice.

Or maybe he awaits his fellow ghosts' arrival on the ghost train that is said to chug into town very late at night, but only during those few weeks when the circus is on its winter hiatus.

For many years, it was possible for ghosts and spirits to wait in comfort in one of two private railroad cars parked on a siding at the old depot, circus historian and Show Folk past president Bob Horne said.

The cars were RB 66 and the JOMAR car. The latter belonged to John and Mable Ringling. It is now in Sarasota, former winter home of the Ringlings. RB 66 belonged to Ringling's most trusted financial officer, Rudy Bundy, known as "Rowdy" to his favorite grandson, Chris Pratt.

Pratt remembers spending his honeymoon on RB 66, next to the Venice train depot.

"That car was down there for years," he said. "It is now in Baraboo with the circus museum (The Circus World Museum in Baraboo, Wisconsin).

The circus and the railroad cars are gone but several performers have chosen to stay in Venice for eternity.

The most notable of the latter is Gunther Gebel Williams, the most famous animal trainer in the world, and, during his colorful career, Venice's favorite son.

Using love and soft words rather than whips and hooks, Gebel Williams managed to have tigers and lions and cheetahs in the same cage with elephants and horses.

In a legendary commercial shot for American Express, he appeared with his favorite cat, a cheetah named Kenny, draped around his shoulders.

As he adopted the Williams name from the famous circus family in which he was raised, Gunther adopted Venice as his home town, dining in its restaurants with his fellow citizens, hosting block parties for his neighbors in the Jacaranda subdivision and attending all sorts of local events when he was not on the road.

He died on July 19, 2001, at the age of 66, and was buried at Venice Memorial Gardens but not before making one final appearance in the center ring at the former circus arena. En route to Our Lady of Lourdes Church where some 2,000 mourners awaited at the invitation-only service, the funeral cortege made a detour to the old circus arena.

His casket was placed in the center ring and draped with a purple and gold performance cape and his favorite cowboy hat, as his family and closest friends gathered for a brief prayer and private goodbye before the public service.

When the lone light that shone on his casket was extinguished, an era had ended.

Yet the memories live on in Venice, as do the haunting sounds of the circus train that many circus fans claim to have heard, even though the tracks have been unused for nearly a decade.

And every year, on Oct 31, precisely at midnight, it is said that a steam locomotive is heard pulling into the Venice depot. It pauses briefly, and then it continues south toward the old circus arena where it has been reported that one can hear the sounds of wild animals echoing through the night.

But only on Oct. 31.

San Marco Hotel gains new guests

$\mathcal{F}$or several years after the Kentucky Military Institute vacated its Venice campus in 1970, the former San Marco Hotel which had housed students for nearly 40 years, sat empty.

It had been easy to transform the old hotel into a dormitory for prep school boys back in 1932. Its neighbor, the old Hotel Venice had been transformed into a classroom building and

67

officer's quarters.

An adjacent smaller building housed the school's commandant, Col. Richmond. Parade grounds and the downtown stores were just across the road.

Richmond had been lured to Venice by a Venice councilman who heard about Richmond's forays into Florida in search of a winter campus for his school. Venice proved to be the ideal location because there was room for a parade ground and two empty hotels sat side-by-side nearly in the heart of town.

Better, yet, the price was right. Venice was very nearly a ghost town and buildings were being sold for about ten percent of what it had cost to build them just four to six years earlier.

Never again, have these buildings been sold for so little, even when destiny caused them to stand empty again for several years.

The first to be sold was the former Hotel Venice. It was to be transformed into an apartment building for senior citizens and then eventually into an assisted living facility.

Richmond's former house was turned into condos. Condo residents share the use of the pool in a hedged and fenced courtyard on the property.

Last to be acquired was the old San Marco Hotel. Eventually it was purchased by Venice undertaker David Farley and three business partners. They planned to restore the Mediterranean Revival building as soon as they could get rid of the transients who had taken up residence throughout the circa 1927 edifice.

"By the time we bought it, it had been filled with

Photo by Kim Cool

The Venice Center Mall is the latest incarnation of what was considered the Best-built building in 19126 Venice when it was known as the San Marco Hotel. Its halcyon days lasted all of about two years before the Florida land boom of the 1920s came to a screeching halt. For more than two years, the former hotel sat empty until the arrival of Col. Charles Richmond, commandant of the Kentucky Military Institute which would give Venice a new lease on life even as Richmond signed the lease on this and the former Hotel Venice. The San Marco was easily transformed into a dormitory. When the KMI vacated Venice in 1971, the building sat vacant again for a few years before being transformed into a retail center with condominium apartments on the upper two floors.

homeless for years," Farley said. "We hired a guard dog company to patrol the building each evening so we could clear them out.

"When that got to be too expensive, I started patrolling the building at night.

"I would walk up the stairs to the third floor (the top floor) and say out loud, 'I am here, with the dogs, and will be checking the building now,' and there would be all sorts of rumbling and scraping noises. Of course, I didn't have any dogs.

"I would walk down the stairs and check each floor and never find anyone. Eventually all would be quiet."

After a few months, there were no more transients, he said.

He never saw anyone in the building although he had always heard the rumblings and scrapings after making his nightly statement.

Perhaps the transients had been very good at hiding themselves.

Perhaps the sounds were just the normal sounds of an old building shuttering in the wind.

Or, maybe the sounds belonged to some other kind of being. Farley never did find out.

He and his partners sold the building a short time later because the restoration costs had proved to be too high, he said.

The next buyer finished the restoration job. Today, the building has retail shops along the avenue on the ground floor and condominiums on the top two floors.

But, late at night, several of the present residents claim to have heard strange noises.

Are the noises being made by former hotel guests, by former students or just the sound of the wind in a 75-year-old building?

Lookout
at the Outlook

$\mathcal{J}$ust across the Intracoastal Waterway from the old Venice train depot is a plain little peach-hued stuccoed building.

Recently it was treated to a fresh coat of peach-hued paint, including a coat of trim paint around windows and doorways in a different shade of peach, a warm tone similar to the colors used on most of the Mediterranean Revival buildings found throughout Venice.

What sets this structure apart from other Venice buildings is its prime loca-

tion along the waterway and its skewed and somewhat trapezoidal shape that evolved from its placement at a 45-degree angle on its site.

Within the one-story building are three small businesses and one bar, The Outlook.

If you have seen one neighborhood watering hole, you have seen the Outlook.

This is a bare bones sort of place, bare bones furniture, plain Jane juke box, four plain television sets.

Food is not on the menu. There is no menu.

There are no plants, no brass rails.

This is where the working folk come for their shots and beers. Until recently, that is all who came to this bar.

It is unlikely that any of the drinks would ever be served with a parasol or other trimming. They don't order Guinness or Harp. These are Busch and Bud drinkers and they show up every day, day in and day out, like their favorite waitress, Tammy. Tammy has been working there for 18 years, according to the bar's manager, Kathy Meinhart.

There may have been some arguments over the years, even a barroom brawl.

What there never had been, until the month of April in the year 2002, was someone so transparent and spirited as the visitor who happened on the scene at closing one night.

Yet that is what Tammy reported.

It was a Thursday night and she was locking up.

She turned off the juke box.

She switched off the television sets, she flipped the switch to douse the lights, and she headed out the door.

Then, as she put her key in the lock, the juke box started to play, the television sets turned themselves back on and every light in the place started to put forth an eerie glow.

Photo by Kim Cool

Sited on a 45-degree angle to the adjacent streets, Venice Avenue East and Tampa Avenue West, the building housing The Outlook neighborhood bar is distinctive for its shape as much as for its longevity. On at least one occasion, the spirited activity within the bar is thought to have given way to spirits which had nothing to do with the imbibing of spirits.The George Kumpe Bridge (known as the Venice Avenue Bridge) is in the background, at a 45-degree angle.

Tammy said there is no master switch that she might accidently have tripped and if there had been, she could not have accidently hit it as she was outside, locking the door when these things happened.

Nevertheless, she went back inside to see what happened and to turn things off again.

Little did she know that, as soon as she re-entered the bar, she would find the solution right before her very eyes.

At the back of the room, near the bar, was a male form.

Actually it was the transparent somewhat shadowy form of a man, eerily floating near the bar.

But it was all the explanation she needed before she hurried out the door and locked the mystery visitor inside.

The visitor must have been equally afraid for when the daytime crew arrived the next morning, the mystery man had left — one way ... or another.

Cheers......

Hungry haunters

One of the most historic buildings in Venice has been so much more than a family homestead.

The present home of Luna Ristorante has a colorful history as well as something that goes bump in the night in the new millennium.

Built in 1926-1927, the two buildings on the site now called the Golden Triangle once housed the first post office in the city, the first bank, the first gener-

al store, the first bed and breakfast, the first kindergarten and possibly the first restaurant, present restaurant owner Mike Altieri said. It continues to be owned by members of the Siede family although the present owners no longer live in Venice.

"This room was the bank vault," he said of the room that now houses the bar area and a few booths in Luna's.

Altieri leases both commercial buildings. His winter restaurant manager, Jimmy "Moon" Mullins, lives in an apartment in the second building. A second apartment also is leased out and the remaining space is used by the restaurant for storage, he said.

"The Siedes still have post office box number one," Altieri said. "That goes back to the days when the grandmother of the present Siedes was the first postmistress in Venice."

Luna Ristorante is at least the third restaurant on the property and those three have all favored Italian food. Both buildings are the classic Northern Italian, Mediterranean Revival-style specified by the Nolen plan for Venice. Altieri also owns Luna's Pizza at the Venice VIllage Shoppes well south of town. Both feature wall-to-wall posters, autographed photos and framed mementoes of the sports and entertainment worlds. A pair of shoes worn by Robert Redford in the film, "The Sting," is but one example. Shelves near the ceiling are filled with lucite display boxes that hold NFL football helmets, autographed game balls and many baseball hats. The bright blue walls can barely be seen for all the framed posters and photographs that have been mounted side-by-side and from top to bottom.

In one room, even the ceiling has been covered with framed items.

Photo by Kim Cool

Situated on the Golden Triangle in Venice, at the corner of North Nokomis and West Tampa avenues, Luna Ristorante serves customers in the building on the right, above. Mysterious sounds emanate from the building on the left, but only in the middle of the night.

When the place is busy — and it usually is, there is barely room to fit the giant serving platters on the tables. What there is no room for is ghosts.

Or, is there?

How much room do shadows, spectres and assorted entities take up anyway?

Bumps in the night take up even less space.

"The strange sounds are upstairs in the other building," Altieri said. "They began about four years ago and occur at random intervals.

"Moon came into work one morning and said he had not slept all night because it sounded like someone was moving furniture upstairs. No one has lived upstairs since 1972 when the last Siede moved out.

"We have since cleaned the space out and there is no furniture up there, just a stove from the 1960s and some storage."

Yet the sound of furniture being moved across the floor can still be heard in the middle of the night, Altieri said. Both Mullins and another tenant have heard the creaky, raking sounds that occur only between 2 and 4 a.m. and never on any sort of schedule.

There is a wood floor on the second floor and no air conditioning which might explain the sounds in the night. The building is basically as it was when completed in 1927.

Is there a logical explanation for these sounds? None that Altieri can come up with.

And with such a checkered history, any number of beings might have returned to the building — a banker, a kindergarten teacher, a cook, a shop keeper, even an inn keeper, any one of whom may need to move some furniture around to restore order to his or her business.

On the other end of the island part of Venice, at the Goldrush BBQ, restaurant owners Bob Overholser and

Patrick Caudhill experienced something totally different at their restaurant.

Instead of strange sounds, there were several strange happenings, always at the same table and with far more regularity than the nocturnal noises at Luna's.

The strange happenings at Goldrush began to occur shortly after the restaurant's opening in 2001.

"People who sat at table 10 were always complaining," Overholser said. "It was always little things, but always something."

Photo by Kim Cool

Table 10 at the Goldrush Barbecue in Venice was either hexed or haunted until the day a restaurant employee decided to take the matter into her own hands.

There was too much salt, not enough salt, they wanted a different salad dressing, they wanted more BBQ sauce on their turkey legs, they didn't have enough moist towelettes - little complaints but always just at this table.

This went on for several weeks. Finally, employee Therese Renuart began to think that table was haunted or hexed, Overholser said.

She decided to do something about it.

The next day she came into the restaurant with a candle which she placed on the table and lit.

According to information in "The Encyclopedia of Ghosts and Spirits," by Rosemary Ellen Guiley, candles were used as early as 3000 B.C. in Egypt and Crete, to repel evil spirits.

Was the table haunted?

Or was there a severe case of bad karma there, drawing unhappy, disturbed and possibly even evil people to that particular table.

If the latter possibility is true, it might explain the presence of one especially evil being who dined at that table one time before the candle was lit . Consider that the candle burning occurred before Sept. 11, 2001.

The evil diner was Mohammed Atta, one of the two terrorists who trained at Huffman Aviation at the Venice Municipal Airport for the airline attack on the World Trade Center that fateful day.

Overholser said that Atta had sat at that table on the one and only time that he came into the restaurant.

In any event, since the day the candle burned itself out, there have been no more strange occurrences at table 10, Overholser said.

The same cannot be said about a third Venice area restaurant, Pelican Alley, on Albee Road, north of Venice, and east of the bridge that leads to Casey Key.

Several employees have said the building is haunted by the ghost of a previous owner.

Even when the wind is still, the front door is said to open and close by itself as footsteps are heard coming and going through the doorway. Occasionally, service items are rearranged without help.

Perhaps he wants to make sure that things are still done his way.

Or maybe, the spirit of Pelican Alley is just hungry. It may have been years since he had a good meal.

Closure

$\mathcal{F}$ew people hear more ghost stories than the local mortician.

Venice undertaker David Farley is no exception.

Farley can be credited with being the first to report to this writer on what may have been Venice's first recognized ghost — the ghost rider of Center Road.

Since then, he has learned of many others.

"There are lots more stories," he said.

Like his father before him, Farley has been in the funeral business for a long time. He has counseled many people in their time of grief following the death of a loved one.

To help them seek closure, he often recommends that the survivors have a final viewing of the deceased before cremation or burial.

One customer, a well-educated and well-read lady, had other ideas.

When her husband passed away, she called Farley to pick up the body and she gave Farley very specific instructions for its disposition.

He was to dress the body of the departed in a special oriental robe that she provided, place the deceased in the finest wood casket available and then to cremate everything. She said she would pay him the following week.

"That will be fine," Farley responded.

He picked up the body, selected the casket and then called the woman to inquire about whether or not she wanted a viewing before the cremation.

"There will be no viewing," she said.

Farley suggested that she and her daughter might find closure more readily if they viewed the body one last time but she would have none of it.

"I know what I am doing," she said.

The mortician scheduled the cremation for the following day.

Before the scheduled time, he received a phone call from the widow.

"I have changed my mind," she said. "My daughter, my housekeeper and I will come to the funeral home this morning to see my husband."

The three mourners showed up a

short while later. After the viewing, and before they left the home, Farley asked the widow what made her change her mind.

"My husband was a man of ritual," she said. "Each night he would watch the news and the weather on television.

"After the weather was over, he would walk out to the beach for awhile and then come back in, go straight to the kitchen and fix a sandwich and drink a glass of milk. Then he would get ready for bed and call for me to join him in the bedroom.

"Last night, my daughter, the housekeeper and I were watching the news. When the weather segment ended, we heard a door open and then close. We huddled a little closer together on the couch, unsure about what to do. A few minutes later, we heard the same door open and close again and we huddled closer still.

"Finally, I got up to check to see if the doors were all closed. When I went into the kitchen, there were sandwich crumbs on the kitchen counter and a glass with the residue of cold milk in the sink.

"That is why we came in today. I don't know what happened, but I know what we heard and what we saw."

Perhaps the widow's husband wanted to send her a message.

Or, maybe he was just hungry.

Old habits die hard.

One of the first hotels built by the Brotherhood of Locomotive Engineers in Venice, circa 1925, was the Hotel Venice on Nassau Street. In 1932, it was given a second chance as the administration and classroom building for the Kentucky Military Institute which had moved its winter quarters to Venice that year, with 150 students. When the KMI left Venice in 1971, the building sat vacant for nearly four years until it was renovated for its third life as a senior citizens' home, Park Place. In the 1990s, the concept was changed yet again and Park Place became an assisted living facility.

Photos by Kim Cool

KMI band members assemble for a year book picture in the 1930s.
below, a KMI pennant,circa 1935.

Back to school

$\mathcal{V}$enice had 60 students in its first school back in 1926.

By 1932, the population of the entire town had shrunk to 400. The school was as empty as the town.

When the Kentucky Military Institute, a boys' prep school located in Lindon, Ky., came to the rescue, with some 150 students that first year, things began to look up.

The KMI students would arrive by

train, just after the New Year, and return to Lindon, Ky. , each April.

Several parents and grandparents followed them to Venice. Some purchased winter homes in the city. Growth was not as rapid as it had been in 1926-27, but for the first time in four years, the city's recovery at last seemed likely.

The KMI cadets became an important asset of the town, drawing crowds to the parade grounds every other Sunday when they would march across the vast green field, in their full dress uniforms.

The military school remained in Venice for nearly 40 years, and many KMI graduates found their way back to Venice years later.

KMI graduate Fred Francis moved to Venice and became the owner of BW Francis (a womens clothing store) in the 1950s. Others came for vacations or when they reached retirement age.

The KMI had saved the town but the town would be unable to save the school.

The school closed its Venice campus in 1970 and, in 1972, ceased to exist entirely. The Lindon campus has been turned into a nursing home and little remains in Venice except a memorial near the old parade grounds and some memorabilia in the Venice Centre Mall.

Yet one person said that a student still remains in Venice, possibly still prowling the halls of the old dormitory, or visiting a former classroom, a student who never graduated.

The story was recounted by a woman who worked in one of the former school buildings until about 10 years ago.

"I always used the stairs on my nightly rounds," she said. "I was in every corner of the building. I never saw anything out of the ordinary, but one of the cooks did."

According to the tale, the cook had gone into the pantry to get a bag of flour. When she opened the door, she found a young man huddled in the corner, wearing a blue military uniform such as those worn by the KMI cadets.

When the cook asked the young man what he was doing there, he turned toward her but said nothing. His horrific countenance was statement enough.

Suddenly afraid, the cook left to seek help.

When she returned, the frightening young man had vanished. He was never seen again, according to the lady who reported the story. She said she thought the cook might have been nipping the cooking sherry.

But then she recounted a second story that may or may not be related to the first.

She said that one year, when the students were being taken back to Kentucky on the train, one of the cadets became very ill.

He was removed from the train and brought back to Venice to be cared for by his grandmother until he would be well enough to travel.

Despite her ministrations, that day never came. The young man died in Venice.

Could he be the same young man who was cowering in the pantry?

Was he looking for his classmates?

Was he hoping to find his way back to Kentucky?

Red marks the spot

Within hours of completing the closing on her 1960s-era house on Glen Oak Road in Venice Gardens, Linda Whitman received an extra piece of paper.

It was in the house, on the kitchen counter. She found it when she did her first walk through as the home's new owner.

The paper was a death certificate, issued in the name of the home's first occupant.

"He had shot himself," Whitman said. "It was very strange to walk in and find that on the kitchen counter, saying he had died of a gunshot wound."

Despite the odd circumstance, she paid no more attention to that incident until she had moved in to the house and long since forgotten the first owner's real name.

But then a string of strange occurrences caused her

to give the man a name, right or wrong. She called him Ralph and decided that for some reason, he or his spirit had decided to return to the house.

One day there was an unexplained puddle in the middle of the floor in the breakfast area. There was no leaky pipe above and nothing had been spilled, Whitman said.

That incident too was put out of her mind, until she painted the kitchen sometime later.

After she completed the job and was cleaning up, red streaks began to appear on one wall.

"It looked like blood," Whitman said. "I wondered if he had died in the kitchen.

"The wall with the streaks was the wall nearest to where the puddle had been. It was next to the garage, in the breakfast area."

On another occasion, Whitman's daughter walked into the bedroom and all of a sudden she could feel the hair on her arms standing up. No sooner had that happened then the bathroom door slammed shut and locked itself.

"I had to get a pin to unlock it," she said. "There was no breeze and the door locks from the inside but there was no one in there."

By this time, Whitman was saying "Ralph is acting up again," naming and blaming the pesky poltergeist.

Both the bathroom and the bedroom doors have closed and locked themselves several times since that first time, she said.

On another occasion, her daughter had acquired a new car, put it in the garage and a half hour later discovered the car's interior light was still on. As she walked toward the car to turn it off, the light went off on its own.

Normally, the light goes off about a minute after the car is parked and turned off, Whitman said. There was no logical explanation for the light to stay on for a half hour - unless "Ralph" had something to do with it.

"Every once in a while you get the feeling that someone or something is there," she said. "My daughter gets the feeling more than I do and so does the older dog. The puppy does not seem to react as much."

No one in the family has seen Ralph but they are very sure he shares the house with them. Even more convinced is a young friend of the family who was at the house a few years ago for a birthday party.

She saw Ralph's reflection in the hall mirror. Yet there was no one near her to be reflected in the mirror.

Was she spooked? Yes.

Was Ralph in the mirror?

Whitman thinks so. Do you?

The story on the following pages was actually the first ghost story penned for this book.

Lingering over dessert with a group of friends who were seated at my dining room table, I mentioned my plan to write "Ghost Stories of Venice." The guests included three of the most well-known ladies in Venice, ladies who, in turn, know just about everyone in town.

It seemed like a good place to begin my quest and, as it turned out, two of them, Ruth and Peaches, the widow of this book's first spirit, shared the haunting experience which follows.

While it did not involve a haunted house or historic figure in the historic town of Venice, it was a start, and, while I did not recognize it at the time, it also offered a clue that the ghost stories of Venice would be different.

Not with my car you won't

The premise of the old 1960s era TV sitcom, "My Mother the Car," was that Jerry Van Dyke's mother, played by Ann Sothern, had returned to earth as his car, following her death. The car would speak only to the son. The story line may have contributed to the show's early demise.

Something very similar occurred in Venice, Florida, a few years back. In the weeks following the death of Rick, several people had occasion to drive his car.

It was one of the best that Detroit had to offer, loaded with all the bells and whistles — power windows, seats, door locks, trunk release, antenna.

The car's electronic gadgetry operated perfectly, when the car was driven by the widow. Unlike non-electric seats that occasionally slip if not pushed into the right groove, the electrically operated seats in Rick's car had always been reliable.

One day, Ruth, the widow's best friend, got behind the wheel, pushed the buttons to slide the front seat into her comfort zone, shifted the gears into drive, and headed down the road.

Less than a block from the house, she heard a slight whirring sound and the seat began to return to the position it had been in when she first got behind the wheel. Ruth had not touched any of the buttons that were needed to operate the seat, beyond her initial adjustments, nor had anything bumped against the buttons.

Thinking that the seat had not caught, even though it was electrically operated, Ruth readjusted the seat to her needs.

A short time later, the whirring noise began and again the seat returned to its starting position.

Despite the annoyance of the moving seat, Ruth finished her errand, returned the car and told her friend that something must be wrong with the seat's motor because each time she adjusted the seat, the seat would seemingly readjust itself.

The widow drove the car the next day, adjusting it for herself. She had no problem. The seat stayed exactly where she put it.

Then, her son took the car out for a ride. He got into the car, inserted the key, adjusted the seat electrically and backed out of the drive onto the road.

As it had the first time Ruth drove the car following

Rick's death, the seat readjusted itself and the gentle whirring noise of the seat's motor could just barely be heard.

As before, the seat continued to readjust itself every time he attempted to move the seat to fit his needs as a driver.

For the next few weeks, the widow was the only one to drive the car and there were no more problems.

To make sure, she did have a mechanic look things over. He could find nothing wrong.

"Rick did not want anyone to drive that car but me," the widow said about Rick and the seat moving incidents that occurred when anyone else would set out to drive the car.

Was Rick sending a message, using the car as a medium?

Ruth is convinced of it. So is Rick's wife who said she experienced another electrical phenomenon a few months later while dining at home with her children.

During the meal, the dining room's chandelier flashed on briefly. No other lights in the house flickered at the time, and the wall switch which operated the chandelier remained in the off position. It was still light outside, too early to turn on the ceiling fixture.

At the time the light flashed, they had been discussing the strange occurrences in Rick's car.

Ghost cowhand

*T*he biggest ranch in the vicinity of Venice is the Taylor Ranch - 15,000 acres big and mostly undeveloped.

Cows roam over most the land, including the 400-acre orange grove and they have for years. This is a working ranch, with cowboys. Most of them also have been there for years, watching out for the land and the cattle.

Some of the land is under development of late. The Taylor Ranch School is there, a church, a Wal-Mart, Books-A-Million, A Hess station, the Women's Resource Center and even a junior college and housing development. All these things take very little of the total acreage so it is easy enough for one cowboy to keep track of these new buildings.

Not that any living cowboy has been assigned to keep track of any of this commercial property.

Instead, it seems as though one cowboy who no longer lives on the ranch (or any other place for that matter) has decided to keep a nightly vigil.

Several people who work in the new office buildings have seen him, but only when they are working late at night.

And none of these people was willing to allow their name or the address of the exact building to be used out of the fear that clients might be upset.

In amassing these stories, that is something I ran into. People are either very willing to talk about ghosts or spirits or energy forces, or they are very reticent. In Venice, there are far more of the latter.

In the case of the cowboy, I spoke with several ladies who had seen him but none wanted her name used.

"We saw him in both buildings," one said. "He was an elderly gentleman, dressed like a cowboy of the 1950s, jeans, hat and shirt."

In each case, he never showed up before 9:30 p.m. Sometimes, no one saw him but they heard him or strange things happened, again, always after 9:30 p.m.

One night, one of the ladies said she knew he was there because she had heard a noise so she closed her door.

"If it's an intruder, he will know where I am because I closed the door," she said that she thought to herself.

But she had little to fear from her ghostly intruder that night.

She called maintenance as soon as she retreated into her office, and when the maintenance man arrived, they found a TV that had been knocked off a stand but the stand was still upright.

"He said that nothing happened and that no one had broken in," she continued, "but the TV was on the floor."

Sometime later, her assistant was working late on a Saturday, finishing up a special project.

She had been making white copies for her department and she heard the copy machine running by itself in the other room. When she went to check on the sound, she found the machine printing out yellow copies.

"Her department always makes white copies," she said. "The other department always makes yellow copies."

There was no one in the building from that or any other department. The selection of yellow paper had not been made by any living person, she said.

"It must have been the cowboy," she said. "Usually he only wanders the halls and nothing happens except when someone is there too late."

Since cowboys generally arise very early, perhaps he was sending a message that these late night workers should go home so they too can get up early the next morning.

Geronimo was a snowbird

For 1,000 years or more, southwest Florida was inhabited only by native Americans, primarily members of the Calusa tribe in the Venice area.

That changed after the pioneers and homesteaders settled the west coast of the state in the latter half of the 19th century.

Then it was only a matter of time before Apache warriors, including the famous Geronimo, were brought into Florida. As the Apaches were hunted

down, many fled to the Sierra Madre Mountains in Mexico. Geronimo managed to elude capture for some 10 years but eventually surrendered and was shipped to Florida with some 300 members of his tribe.

One of Geronimo's people is still in the area, grumbling about the family that built a home on "his land," according to Pat Charnley, the founding minister of the Angel Ministry Church in Venice.

She was calling on one of her parishioners when she found the apache spirit in the home, she said.

"He did not realize he was dead," she said.

The snowbird returned

*P*eggi Paquette's parents were part-time Venice residents. They came each winter from Sharon, Pa.

They owned a house in Venice Gardens, a development of homes built just east of the Venice City limits in the early 1960s, during the third incarnation of the city that refused to become a ghost town.

Venice had boomed a second time during World War II when the United States Army built a military airport at the southern-most part of the land area that had been platted by city planner John Nolen back in the 1920s.

Venice's population had nearly doubled, from 400 in 1930 to more than 700 residents when the 1950 census was taken. While still not approaching its high of some 4,000 residents in 1928, the city's ranks would surpass that number before the 1960 census.

Many of these new residents were, like Paquette's parents, "snowbirds." The term is used to define people who come each winter to spend a few weeks or months basking in the warm Florida sun before returning to their northern homes. They are revered by shopkeepers and hoteliers and reviled by those who must wait an hour or more to be served at their favorite eatery because it is filled with the "snowbirds."

Venice Gardens was an ideal housing development for both snowbirds and year-round residents. Sporting names like "The Orchid," two-bedroom, two-bath model homes sold for prices that averaged less than $12,000 including lot, on a palm-lined street, not too far from the Venice beach. Venice Gardens' community center included an Olympic-sized swimming pool, tennis courts, shuffleboard and other amenities. Those who wanted their own pool could have one for about $3,000.

Boom times were returning to Venice.

Boo times were yet to come.

Peggi took a teaching job in Venice in the late 1970s, soon after graduating from college.

Her parents celebrated the birth of their grandson Paul a few years later and spent longer vacations in Venice until 1998 when Paquette's father died in Pennsylvania. He was buried in Sharon, Pa.

Two of his chairs were given to his daughter. One was his favorite recliner.

When Paquette's only son reached college age, she decided to downsize and moved from her large house to a condo, taking the two chairs along. She settled in and began to adjust to an empty nest as Paul headed off to college in Connecticut for his freshman year.

Nothing unusual happened until the end of Paul's Christmas break .

Mother and son were in the condo's living room. She was seated on her father's recliner.

"I felt a presence in the room," she said. "And when it vanished, the scent of my father remained.

"You know how everyone has a distinct aroma," she continued. "Well, I just knew that that scent was my father."

This event happened about 9:30 p.m. on a Wednesday evening. Thursday, at 7:30 a.m., about the time that Paquette was leaving for school, it happened again, she said. There was the distinct odor that she said reminded her of her father. When she returned home at 5:30 p.m., there was a third "visit."

"I could sense he was there," she said. "Paul didn't notice anything and thought I was being silly."

The odor might have come from the recliner but Paul did not smell it and Paquette's father had been gone long enough that any residual odor should have disappeared.

Paquette went to the grocery store later than evening.

"When I came out of Publix, I sensed that he was there too," she said.

These events occurred just about the time of year when the snowbirds begin arriving in Florida as her father once had.

"I know he was here," she said.

Is it or is it not?

There always has to be at least one exception to every rule.

And so it is with the photos in this book.

With one exception, all the photos in this book depict places that may or may not be haunted. With one exception, the photos contain images that can be readily explained. With one exception, there are no visible spirits in any of the photos.

That one exception is the photo which accompanies this brief chapter. It was taken in April, 2001 during services

Photo by Anthony Salerno

Members of the Church of the Angels in Venice, Fla. believe they were visited by an angel in April 2001. Church founder, Patricia Charnley, said that the two shadowy shapes on the left half of this photo are the wings of an angel and that the dark round area between the wings is the angel's head.

at the Church of the Angels in Venice. Anthony Salerno was photographing the speaker on the podium. He took several pictures to make sure he would have at least one good shot to take with him on a trip north the following week.

When he went to collect the developed pictures at the drugstore, he saw that all the pictures were crisp and clear, with one exception, near the end of the roll. That one photo contained what Salerno at first thought was the shadowy image of a ghost.

"I only saw the image to the right," he said. "At first, I didn't notice the similar image to the left."

The two images, when viewed together, appear to be angel wings, Salerno said.

To Pat Charnley, the founder of the Angel Ministry Church, there is nothing unusual about seeing an angel in the sanctuary. What is unusual is that the image was captured on film, she said as she showed this writer the negative and several enlargements of the original photo.

Perhaps Salerno was at the right place at the right time to capture a form of ectoplasm or an apparition and not a sun spot, wisps of smoke or glare from the lights in the church.

Charnley is convinced of it.

What do you think?

Is that all?

Perhaps.

And then again, when it comes to things that go bump in the night, who knows?

As this book was being completed, Venice was celebrating its 75th anniversary in a state which had been settled more than 400 years earlier by Spanish explorers and which had been populated by Native Americans for at least 1,000 years before that.

Stories of ghosts, spirits, spectres

and other haunting types are nearly as prolific on the east coast of Florida as they are in the mists of Scotland, Ireland or Wales.

Things seem to be different on Florida's west coast and so too are its ghosts and legends.

But, thanks to those generous folks who shared their tales, the first stories have been penned.

Will there be more?

For this writer, the "haunt" along the Gulf Coast continues. If you have a ghostly tale to share about any area of the Gulf Coast of Florida, please contact Kim Cool by e-mail at: kimcool@historicvenicepress.com or at Historic Venice Press, P.O. Box 800, Venice, FL 34284.

Photo by Marianna Csizmadia

About the author

*T*he author is new to the realm of ghost hunting but not to writing and not to being tenacious. Kim Cool has written business books and needlecraft books in another life.

In this life, the Sweet Briar College graduate writes about Venice, entertainment, homes and travel as the Features Editor of the *Venice Gondolier Sun*. She also is a member of the Venice Archives and Area Historical Collection, the Venice Historical Society, the Advisory Board of the Salvation Army of Venice, a national synchronized, senior competition and gold test judge for the United States Figure Skating Association, a former competitive curler at the national level and a charter member of the Florida Curling Club.

Raised in Shaker Heights, Ohio, she now resides in Venice, Florida.

Acknowledgments

This book would not have been written without the help of those who shared their stories, those who put me in touch with those generous people and those who read the prepublication tales. Still others were helpful just because they were there to lend an ear and to offer moral support. To all, including the ghosts who were willing to be seen or experienced, thank you.

The ghosts:
Only the spirits know for sure who they are, or ... were.

The people:
Charles J. Adams III, Michael Altieri, Irv Armbruster aka Amtrak the Clown, Geri Becker, Doug Bolduc, Pat and Trevor Charnley, Murray Chase, Rollins Coakley, Mariana Csizmadia, Ruth Ann Dearybury, Sam Dillon, Linda Fagan, David Farley, Rina Farlow, Charles Finley, Sigrid Gebel, Dorothy Grotefent, Peaches Haas, Bob Hakes, Tom Hodgini, Maureen Holland, Bob Horne, Pat Horwell, Pam Johnson, Jackie LeClaire aka The Master of Mirth, Carol Lee, Mary Mancuso, Bob and Melinda Mudge, Laurel O'Connors, Bob Overholser, Peggi Paquette, Spencer Pullen, Chris Pratt, Alvin Schwartz, Anthony Salerno, Jan Stevenson, Scott Strohe III, Alvin Schwartz, Caroll Swayze, Ruth Swayze, Faith and Donald Sweeney, Laura Young Thurman, Nancy Tollsma, Carolyn Tonidandel, Jean Trammell, Fran Valencic, Jenny Wallenda, Linda Whitman, Penny Wilson.

Bibliography

Adams, Charles J. Cape May Ghost Stories, Book III. Exeter House Books. 2002.

Adams, Charles J. New York City Ghost Stories. Exeter House Books. 1996.

Adams, Charles J. Philadelphia Ghost Stories. Exeter House Books. 1998.

An Historical Architectural Survey. Venice, Florida, second printing, 1995.

Blackman, W. Hayden. The Field Guide to North American Hauntings. Three Rivers Press. 1998.

Downer, Deborah. Editor. Classic American Ghost Stories. August House Publishers. 1990.

Guiley, Rosemary Ellen. Ghosts and Spirits, Second Edition. Checkmark Books. 2000.

Hauck, Dennis William. The National Directory Haunted Places, Penquin Books, 1996.

Jones, Richard. Haunted Britain and Ireland. Barnes & Noble Books. 2001.

Matthew, Janet Snyder. Venice, Journey From Horse and Chaise, a History of Venice, Florida. Pine Level Press Inc. 1989.

McSherry, Jr. Frank D.; Waugh, Charles G. Greenburg, Martin H.; editors. Great American Ghost Stories. Rutledge Hill Press.1991.

Mendoza, Patrick M. Between Midnight and Morning, Historic Hauntings and Ghost Tales. August House Publishers Inc. 2000.

Murphy, Douglas R. From Barefoot Boy to Doc ... My Journey. Morningside Press. 2001.

Ogden, Tom. The Complete Idiot's Guide to Ghosts and Hauntings. Alpha Books, a division on Macmillan USA, Inc. 1999.

Turner, Gregg M. Venice in the 1920s. Arcadia Publishing, an imprint of Tempus Publishing. 2000.

Youngberg, George E. Sr. Venice. Sunshine Press.1976.